This book belongs to

. . . .

ISBN 978 1 84939 560 1   ISBN 978 1 84939 760 5 (paperback)

First published in Great Britain in 2013 by Andersen Press Ltd.
20 Vauxhall Bridge Road, London SW1V 2SA.
Published in Australia by Random House Australia Pty.,
Level 3, 100 Pacific Highway, North Sydney, NSW 2060.
Text copyright © Peter Bently, 2013. Illustration copyright © Mei Matsuoka, 2013.
The rights of Peter Bently and Mei Matsuoka to be identified
as the author and illustrator of this work have been asserted by them
in accordance with the Copyright, Designs and Patents Act, 1988.
All rights reserved. Colour separated in Switzerland by Photolitho AG, Zürich.
Printed and bound in Malaysia by Tien Wah Press.

10 9 8 7 6 5 4 3 2 1

British Library Cataloguing
in Publication Data available.

To Lucy,
for the cosmic inspiration.
P. B.

To Uncle Peter,
for encouraging me to
reach great heights.
M. M.

The Great Balloon Hullaballoo

Peter Bently & Mei Matsuoka

ANDERSEN PRESS

Simon the Squirrel
was off to play ball,
But there stood
his mum with a
list in the hall.

"Please pop to the shop, Simon dearest. Here's money
For loo-roll, new pants for yourself, bread and honey.

And one thing that's much
more important than these,
Tonight we've got pizza,
so don't forget CHEESE!"

So off trotted Simon with Rodney Raccoon.
Suddenly Simon said, "Look, it's the Moon!
Everybody knows that it's made out of cheese.
If we jump we can take just as much as we please!"

They ran to the lake in a mad gleeful dash,
Leapt from a tree trunk and landed –

KER-SPLASH!

"You pair of daft noodles! The Moon's in the sky!"
Laughed Bethany Bear, who stood
watching nearby.

"No problem!" said Simon. "We'll FLY to the Moon –

In Old Uncle Somerset's Special balloon!"

"You're all very welcome to go for a ride,"
Said Old Uncle Somerset. "Clamber inside!
Grab a nice cushion. There's plenty to try."
Then he untied the rope and they rose in the sky!

They shot into space with spectacular force

Until a great comet –

WHOOOOOSH!

–blew them off course!

"You've gone the wrong way!"
said a cow with a frown
(She had just jumped the Moon
and was on her way down.)

"Oh well," Simon said,
as they sped through
the stars,

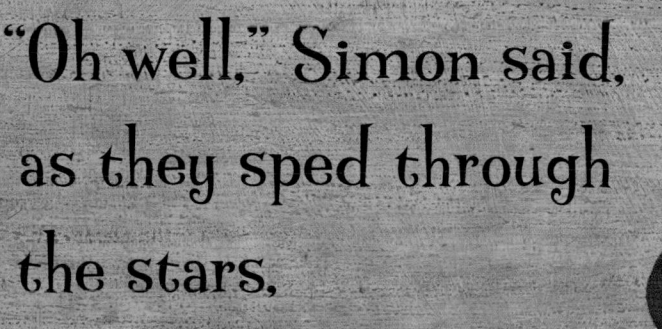

"It looks like
we'll have to go
shopping on Mars!"

They landed on Mars and bought honey and bread

From a little green man with three eyes in each head.

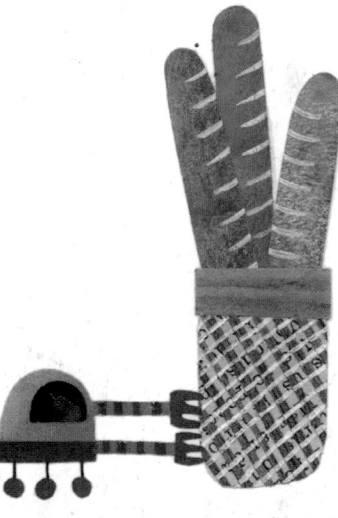

Bethany called to her friends: "Look at me!

There's a wonderful view from this funny old tree.

But why is it covered in

hairy pink moss?"

They fled from the monster and headed for Saturn,
Where Simon tried pants with a star-spangled pattern.

"Look at that weirdo!" the aliens said.
(On Saturn they all wear their pants on their head.)

At the store on Uranus, all shrouded in mist,
Simon said, "Toilet roll's next on Mum's list!"

"Of course!" grinned the Thing with the tentacled face,
"For loo roll this planet is just the right place!"

"Right," declared Simon. "Before we go back,
Why don't we stop for a drink and a snack?"

They called in at Pluto for cosmic rock cakes,

Which they ate at the Milky Way Parlour with shakes.

On Neptune
they hoped to get space
fish and fries.
Instead all they caught
was a scary surprise!
"Time to head home! Give it

maximum power!"
Said Simon,

then –

They drifted back down to the earth with a

BUMP!

That made Uncle Somerset wake with a jump!

"Oh, don't mind the puncture,"
    he said. "I can patch it.
But you'd better run home to your mum
    or you'll catch it!"

Imagine the look of surprise on Mum's face
When Simon declared, "I've been shopping in space!"
"You can tell us about it at dinner time, please,"
Said his mum. "I've made pizzas. I just need the CHEESE."

Simon searched in the bag for the things on Mum's list.

"Whoops!" blushed the squirrel. "There's one thing I missed . . ."

CHEESE!!!

If you enjoyed this, you'll also love:

9781842709887

9781849393843

9781842705377